SYDNEY SUNSHINE

and the BIG BIRTHDAY BASH

I0692170

by SYDNEY MCGEE

VISIBLE WORKS CHILDREN'S BOOKS

HOUSTON

SYDNEY SUNSINE AND THE BIG BIRTHDAY BASH

Copyright © 2018 by Sydney McGee

For information contact:
Visible Works Publishing
P.O. Box 61101, Houston, TX 77208

ISBN: 978-0984688968

First Edition: July 2018
10 9 8 7 6 5 4 3 2 1

VISIT SYDNEY SUNSHINE

www.sydneysunshine.net

Facebook Page: www.facebook.com/SydSunshine1

Twitter: www.twitter.com/SydSunshine1

Instagram: www.instagram.com/SydSunshine1

YouTube Channel: Sydney Sunshine

Hello!

Friendship plays a big role in life. Friendships teach you about love, earning trust, being loyal, and forgiving others. Friendships are based on being friendly, caring, and treating people with kindness and concern. So, shine bright and be a great friend!

Love,
Sydney Sunshine

This book is dedicated to Aubrey, Christen & Austin.

I am so happy you are my family and my best friends.

I will love you forever.

–Sydney Sunshine

"It's Wednesday!" Sydney yelled.

Sydney Sunshine woke up and jumped out of bed. She had been up all night long thinking about how fun her birthday party was going to be on Saturday and what she would wear.

"It's my birthday and I am excited!"

Today was her actual birthday, and deep down she was happy with joy! Sydney had just turned ten.

Everyone in the family knew that the tenth birthday was extra special.

In her family, when you turn ten, you get to choose the location for your birthday party, and Saturday would finally be her big day! Having a tenth birthday celebration was passed down from generation to generation.

In just two more days, Sydney was going to have a Big Birthday Bash!

Sydney was going to invite fifteen of her friends and classmates. But only five of her friends, all girls, would come to a sleepover Friday night *before* the party. They were going to have so much fun.

Sydney sat on the edge of her bed thinking about all of her birthday plans. She could not wait to have hours of fun with everyone, especially her best friend Isabelle.

Sydney and Isabelle were friends even before they started elementary school.

Sydney liked dogs, Isabelle liked dogs. Sydney loved reading books, Isabelle loved reading books. Sydney's favorite color was pink, Isabelle's favorite color was pink. And there was only one thing that they both disliked... not being able to spend time with each other.

Sydney and Isabelle both knew what it meant to be a good friend. They cared for each other and they were loyal. When one of them felt sad, the other was always there with a big hug and an even bigger smile.

Isabelle and Sydney always spent time together, and on the weekends, they went to places like the mall, the park, or they hung out at each other's home. But, this Friday and Saturday, Isabelle was going to be at the birthday bash!

Sydney thought about how Isabelle was going to love the pink and yellow table covers, balloons, party bags, cake, and the beautiful invitations.

Sydney knew that this would be the best birthday that she would never forget.

Sydney Sunshine got dressed for school. She wore her "TODAY IS MY BIRTHDAY" shirt with some jeans and tennis shoes. She wore her big pink hairbow.

"I'm ready to go to school!" she chanted down the stairs and to the bus.

Sydney Sunshine jumped off the school bus and met her friends in the school hallway. She was laughing and talking all the way into the classroom. Sydney was so excited!

When Sydney got into the classroom, she hurried to her seat because the school announcements were about to begin.

When the announcements blasted through the speakers, all the kids jumped in their seats, especially Sydney.

"Today we have a special birthday in

Mrs. Fall's class. Sydney Sunshine!"

Sydney was sort of embarrassed, but happy at the same time.

"Sydney, come to the front office and get your birthday ribbon."

On the way out the door, Sydney's teacher handed her a small bag of candy. "Hurry, Sydney! Go get your ribbon. Happy Birthday!"

All of the kids burst into cheers and sang Happy Birthday off key and with no harmony at all. The cheers were so loud, Mrs. Hall had to quiet them down.

Isabelle jumped up and gave Sydney a huge hug. "Happy Birthday Best Friend!" Sydney said thanks and ran out of the classroom.

Sydney's bash was off to an awesome start.

Sydney Sunshine had a hard day at school because she wasn't able to focus on her school work, plus after school she had a big task. She had to deliver invitations.

It was hard for Sydney Sunshine to keep the birthday surprise to herself during the day. She wanted to share the details with everyone, but she decided not to ruin all of the fun. Her friends would find out later that day.

Sydney Sunshine got home from school, changed clothes, and began planning her mail route. Sydney's and all of her friends lived on the same street. Sydney was glad because that meant that she could ride her bike. She kissed her mother and headed out to make her deliveries.

Sydney went from one house to another. She opened each mailbox and put the invitation in there flat. She didn't slam it because she didn't want her friends to hear the mailbox door because she wanted it to be a surprise.

She didn't want any of them to come out to see what all the commotion was.

Sydney smiled when she had delivered the last invitation.

She rushed back home so none of her friends would see her or catch her at their house. She was going so fast, it seemed as though the trees were in a race with her. Luckily, Sydney won.

Once inside the house, Sydney sat and laughed at the special invitation delivery. She felt like a real mailman.

Even with all of the fun she had that day, Sydney still had a feeling that she had forgotten something important. She tried to think of what it could be, but her thoughts were replaced with thoughts of her party.

Later that night, Sydney was in her bedroom sitting on her bed and she suddenly remembered that she forgot to make and deliver an invitation to a very special person. Somehow, she had forgotten about her best friend in the whole wide world, Isabelle.

Sydney was disappointed. What was she going to do? She decided that she would deliver Isabelle's invitation to her on Thursday.

The next day after school, Sydney's mother took her to her favorite bakery, Yum Yum's Cakes, to pick out her cake. Sydney knew which one she wanted. It would be vanilla cake with vanilla icing. Sydney knew that Isabelle would like it, too.

Next, Sydney went to the mall to pick out her birthday bash outfit. She found the dress she wanted and matching shoes. She was all ready and soon they were on their way home. She was tired and had a long day.

She changed into her pajamas and went to bed. She felt like she was missing something. "What am I missing? No, I am not forgetting anything."

Sydney closed her eyes. "I can't wait until tomorrow."

Sydney tried drifting off to sleep, but something was bothering her. She could not figure out what it was. That bothered her even more.

She tossed and turned for hours. Then, she fell asleep.

Her dreams were filled with colorful pictures of friends, candy, confetti, balloons, gifts, food, party favors, excitement, excitement, and more excitement!

HAPPY BIRTHDAY SYDNEY!

Sydney had been busy all day Thursday and Friday evening getting prepared for her sleepover and party. Two days had passed, and it was finally time for her party to begin. Sydney felt like she was still forgetting something important. But she could not think of what it was.

Friday night Sydney wondered why Isabelle didn't come to the sleepover. Sydney still didn't remember that she hadn't delivered Isabelle's invitation. She was having a blast.

Sydney and her friends dressed into their pajamas. They had a pillow fight and played board games. They watched three movies and ate popcorn, chips, candy, and drinks.

Afterwards, Sydney's mom spoiled the fun when she yelled, "Time to go to bed."

All of them yelled, "Awwwwwww man!"

"Get into your sleeping bags everybody," said Sydney.

Everyone got into their sleeping bags but couldn't fall asleep because they had such a fun and exciting day.

They sat up and told stories and everyone talked about what they were going to do for their own birthdays.

Finally, Sydney dozed off to sleep, then another and another. Soon all the girls were asleep.

In the morning, at 7:00 a.m. the girls got up, got dressed, and went downstairs to eat breakfast. They had rice, eggs, biscuits, and sausage. It was yummy.

"Your mom makes a good breakfast, Sydney. She should be a chef," said Maria.

Sydney laughed and agreed.

Sydney and the girls ate everything.

After breakfast they went to get their nails and toes painted white, pink and green. They were feeling very girly!

Next, they went to Bouncy Palace, a trampoline park. This is where the actual birthday party was.

There they jumped for three hours and ate pepperoni pizza.

Sydney and her friends bounced and bounced and imagined they were reaching for the sky.

They bounced so much until they were dizzy and bumping into each other.

Sydney fell flat on the trampoline. She was tired. She laid there on her back and had a thought about Isabelle. Sydney became devastated. She finally remembered that she had forgotten to deliver Isabelle's invitation.

Sydney's mother called Sydney and her friends in the party room. It was time to cut the cake and open presents.

Sydney wanted to start with cake first.

Her mother lit the candles, and everyone sang Happy Birthday! Sydney closed her eyes and made a wish. Sydney wished that Isabelle was there at the birthday party.

Sydney's mother sliced the cake and each person got a piece.

Sydney's mother came over to her because she was picking at her slice of cake.

Sydney's mom had a mouthful of cake. Her cheeks were stuffed like a chipmunk.

"What's wrong, Sunshine? It's your birthday!"

"Nothing. I am just sad because Isa..." Sydney's voice trailed off.

"Isabelle what? Tell me, Sydney."

Sydney didn't answer.

As Sydney's mother was leaving the table, Sydney said, "Mom, can you drop me off at Isabelle's house after the party? I need to talk to her, please?"

"Okay, Sunshine." Her mother nodded her head.

Sydney gave her mother a weak smile and went back to nibbling on her cake.

Next, Sydney opened her gifts.

Sydney got every single gift that she'd asked for. A microphone, a dollhouse, a toy puppy, a new bicycle, gift cards, shoes, clothes, and more. But, she was sad because her best friend Isabelle wasn't there to see any of it.

Everyone's parents came to pick them up. Sydney headed home with her gifts, her cake, and her disappointment.

On the way home, Sydney asked her mother to stop by the house. She wanted to change her dress. Then, she asked her mother to take her to the store.

Sydney bought a small pink gift bag, some tissue paper, and something special. Then, they went to Isabelle's house.

Sydney knocked on Isabelle's door. When the door opened, Sydney couldn't even look into Isabelle's eyes. Isabelle frowned and became sad because Sydney was sad.

"Sydney, what's wrong?"

"I wanted to tell you, I forgot to invite you to my birthday party. It was today. You missed all of it and I am really sorry."

Isabelle motioned for Sydney to come inside. They sat on the couch.

"Isabelle, I forgot to deliver your invitation to my birthday bash. I feel so aweful. I am so sorry. Will you forgive me?"

Sydney broke down crying.

Isabelle looked at Sydney with disbelief and she started crying, too.

Sydney wiped her eyes.

"Isabelle, its not because we aren't friends. It's because I was so busy preparing for the sleepover and party. The party was not the same without you being there. You are my best friend. I wanted you there. This was all my fault."

Sydney passed Isabelle a small gift bag. "I bought this for you. It is a symbol of our friendship."

Isabelle gently took the bag from Sydney. She wiped her tears and opened the gift bag.

"It's a bracelet! It's beautiful, Sydney! Thanks so much!"

Sydney heard a car horn. It was her mother letting her know it was time to go.

The girls walked outside together.

"Isabelle, do you want to come over to my house for a mini party? We can stay up late and eat the rest of the cake."

"Yes," shouted Isabelle. "Stay right here while I ask my mom!"

Isabelle ran inside and ran back out jumping up and down as if she were on a pogo stick.

"Let's go!"

The girls jumped into the car and headed to Sydney's house.

Isabelle looked over at Sydney.

"Sydney, I forgive you. We are still best friends."

Sydney closed her eyes and imagined her and Isabelle standing in front of a rainbow and hugging.

Sydney smiled and said, "Yes! We are friends forever!"

ABOUT THE AUTHOR

Sydney McGee (a.k.a Sydney Sunshine) is a ten-year-old, super silly, and fun girl. Known for her wild, make-believe characters and one-of-a-kind storytelling, her love for bringing stories to life is what led her to become a published author.

Where did she get her name? Sydney was penned with the name "Sydney Sunshine" at age five. Her teachers felt that her bubbly and lively personality deserved a name that reflected how she begins each school day with hugs and happiness. Sydney has a way of making others smile. Known for being respectful, polite, and joyful, Sydney is everyone's friend. From this, the name Sydney Sunshine was born and has followed her throughout elementary school. An honor roll student, Sydney loves Math and Language Arts.

Sydney loves theater and has performed in various dramatizations and plays. When she is not writing or acting, she is spending time with her friends, family, and her dog, Nadya.

In the Sydney Sunshine book series, Sydney spreads positive messages about morals, values, and personal character development. Her stories teach elementary-age children to be kind, respectful, accepting and loving to self and others. Sydney's signature message to children is to LET YOUR LIGHT SHINE!

Visit Sydney at:

www.sydneysunshine.net

Also in the Sydney Sunshine Series:

A BOOK ABOUT SELF-ESTEEM & SELF-CONFIDENCE

1

SYDNEY SUNSHINE
and the NOT-SO-MAGIC MIRROR

SYDNEY MCGEE
Illustrated by REGINA CARTER

Sydney Sunshine receives a surprise gift—a special mirror with magical powers—that has been handed down from one generation to another. The reflection in the mirror is that of a girl she has never seen before, and the illusions have a positive effect on Sydney Sunshine. But, when something happens to her mirror, she feels hopeless and is left with unanswered questions. Will Sydney Sunshine be able to find the magic within herself? Or, is the magic only inside the little girl she sees in the mirror?

Also in the Sydney Sunshine Series:

A BOOK ABOUT RESPONSIBILTY

SYDNEY SUNSHINE
and HER SUMMER at AUNT JANET'S FARM

#1 National Best Selling Author
SYDNEY MCGEE
Illustrated by REGINA CARTER

Sydney Sunshine is excited about her summer plans—a vacation to her Aunt Janet's farm. Given the responsibility of taking care of the cows, chickens, horses and other animals, Sydney is certain she will make Aunt Janet proud. But, when things don't go as planned and the farm is turned upside down, will Sydney Sunshine be able to fix things and still have a memorable summer or will her time spent on the farm be of memories she'd rather forget?

Thanks for reading! I hope you enjoyed! Please add a short review on Amazon and let me know what you thought!

NEXT IN THE SYDNEY SUNSHINE BOOK SERIES

SYDNEY SUNSHINE
and the Mysterious Big Harvey
A book about compassion and kindness

www.ingramcontent.com/pod-product-compliance
Lightning Source LLC
Chambersburg PA
CBHW041030170626
46815CB00001B/29

9780984688968